P9-DET-609

The Orphans of Normandy

This book is for you,
Aunt Aggie, and for
the orphans of Normandy.
Love, Nancy

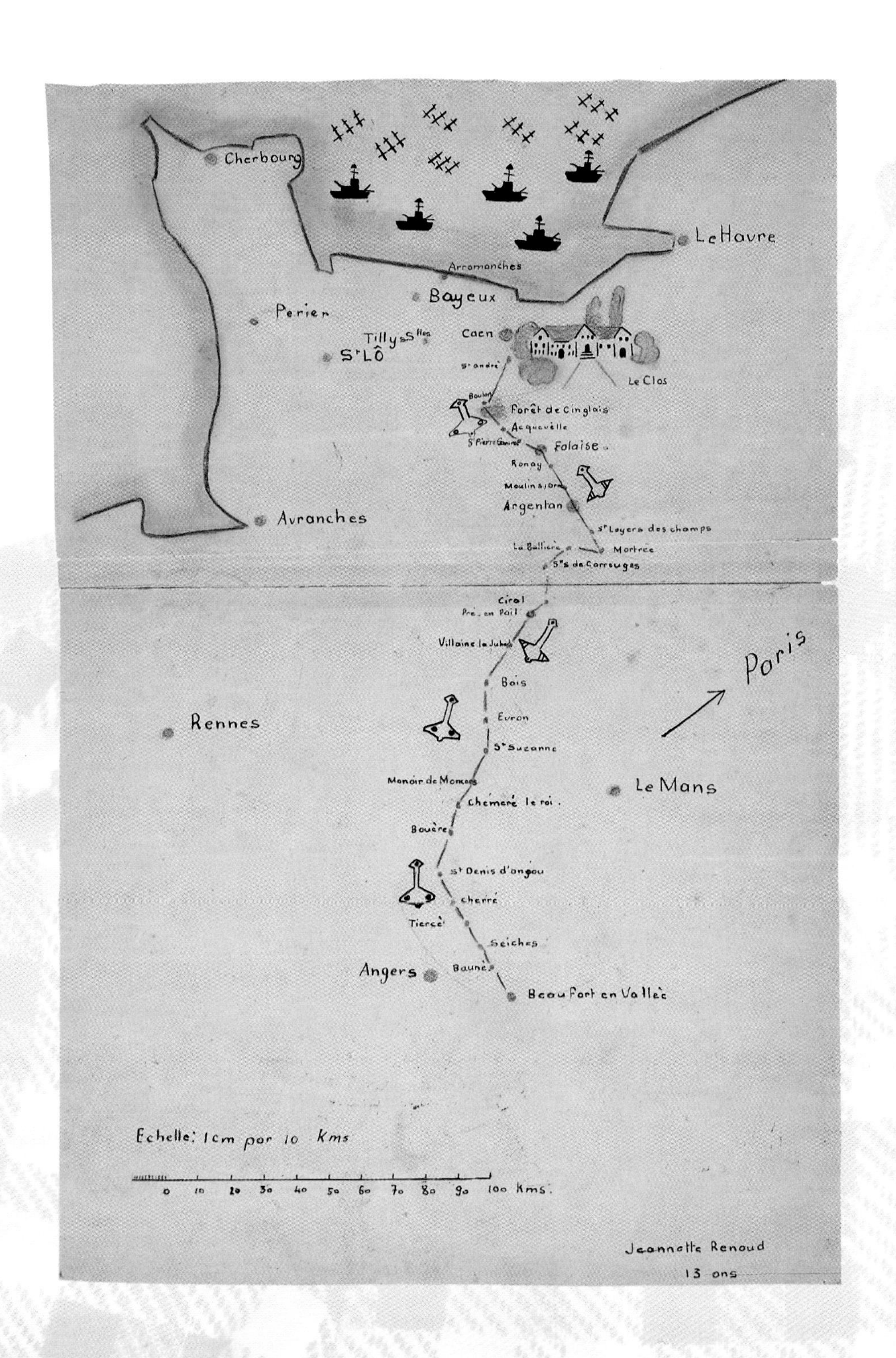

The Orphans of Normandy

A true story of World War II told through drawings by children

NANCY AMIS

ATHENEUM BOOKS FOR YOUNG READERS

New York London Toronto Sydney Singapore

Atheneum Books for Young Readers
An imprint of Simon & Schuster Children's Publishing Division
1230 Avenue of the Americas, New York, New York 10020

Book design by Ann Bobco
The text of this book is set in
Granjon Bold and Blockhead Unplugged.
The illustrations are rendered in colored pencil on newsprint.
Manufactured in China
First Edition
1 2 3 4 5 6 7 8 9 10
Amis, Nancy
The Orphans of Normandy / Nancy Amis
p. cm.
Summary: Relates how one hundred young schoolgirls, many of them orphans, and their teachers managed to escape the chaos of the Allied invasion of Normandy on June 6, 1944, by taking shelter in an iron mine for thirty-eight days and, after being forced out by the Germans, walking for twenty-nine days to reach safety behind Allied lines.
ISBN 0-689-84143-4
1. World War, 1939–1945 Campaigns—France—Normandy—Juvenile Fiction. [1. World War, 1939–1945 Campaigns—France—Normandy—Fiction. 2. Orphans—Fiction. 3. Survival—Fiction.]
I. Title.
PZ7.R252773 Or 2003
[Fic]—dc21 2002027816

acknowledgments

My great-aunt, Agnes Fulton Amis, went to France in 1919 after World War I. She knew very little French, but learned to speak the language while working among the French people. She attended the Sorbonne and later taught French as an exchange teacher to French children. Through her many friends in France, combined with the efforts of her French students and the American Relief for France, she was able to contribute to building a strong relationship between the United States and France. For her diplomatic accomplishments she was awarded in 1937, and again in 1962, the Cross of Officer from L'Ordre des Palmes Académiques.

Allons, Enfants

On June 6, 1944, one hundred girls walked silently out of their home and into the dark night. The red, white, and blue tattersall dresses that they wore were their only clothes. Some of the girls had no shoes, but they had to escape from the danger of the Allied invasion of Normandy and the German defense against it.

France had been living under German occupation since 1940. The world was at war, families were split apart, and many children were homeless. Before the occupation, La Maison du Clos in St. Andre-sur-Orne was a home and school for girls whose parents could no longer care for them or who had died. By 1944, when France was under German control, there were one hundred girls who lived at the orphanage. Before the bombs began to fall, Mademoiselle LeVallios and the teachers worked hard to provide everything the girls needed for a happy and productive life.

That night everything changed. From their bedroom window, they watched vibrant lights in the sky. Planes were flying overhead. The noise of bombs falling and machine guns rat-a-tat-ting was loud enough that they had to hold their ears closed with trembling hands.

Allons, enfants, vite, vite! We must go! Now! Hurry! Hurry! We must leave our home! *Allons, enfants.* Let's go children. Each girl carried a blanket, a little white flag, and some bread. From La Maison du Clos, they walked down the driveway, through the gate, and slowly, quietly, up the road and over the hill. The journey had begun.

"The Clos, on the banks of the Orne, near Caen, welcomed little girls who were orphans without homes, and prepared them, in a homelike atmosphere, for life. The large estate of twenty-five acres included . . . the residence: kitchen, dining room, dormitories, bathrooms, dressing rooms; the school buildings: kindergarten, primary school, trade schools, and workrooms."

— Nicole Folliot, 13

La maison d'enfants du Clos.
(actuellement réfugiée aux Buissons. Champcueil. Seine.et.Oise)
Le
Clos
situé sur
les bords de
l'Orne, près de Caen,
(actuellement réfugié aux
Vauréal par Cergy
Buissons, à Champcueil. Seine et Oise)
accueillait dès leur plus
jeune âge les petites filles sans foyer et les préparait à la vie dans une atmosphère familiale
Cette grande propriété de 9 hectares comprenait les bâtiments de la maison d'habitation : cui.
sine, réfectoires, dortoirs, lavabos, vestiaires .. les bâtiments scolaires: jardin d'enfants, écoles
Nicole Folliot
13 ans

Spring 1944

"In the schoolroom at the Clos, the little girls from three to fourteen learned their lessons."

— Emma Renad, 19

En classe, au Clos même, les petites filles de 3 à 14 ans étaient instruites.

"The more grown-up girls learned to sew, in the sunny sewing room, overlooking the river."

— Denise Lerossignal, 11

Les petites filles devenues
grandes apprenaient la cou.
ture, dans leur bel atelier
près de l'Orne.
SINGER
Denise Lerossignol
11 ans
IX

"During playtime, in the warm weather, swimming in the cool water of the Orne was wonderful. We dove and dove all day."

– Hélène Han, 12

Aux heures de récréation,
l'été, comme il faisait
bon de se baigner
dans l'eau fraîche
de l'Orne! Les plongeons
n'arrêtaient pas!
Hélène - Han.
12 ans
X

"Gaston, the gardener of the Clos, lovingly tended the big vegetable garden, which provided us with fresh vegetables daily. Oh, the cabbage soups, the tender carrots, and the juicy fruits we enjoyed."

– Jacqueline Lacaz, 10

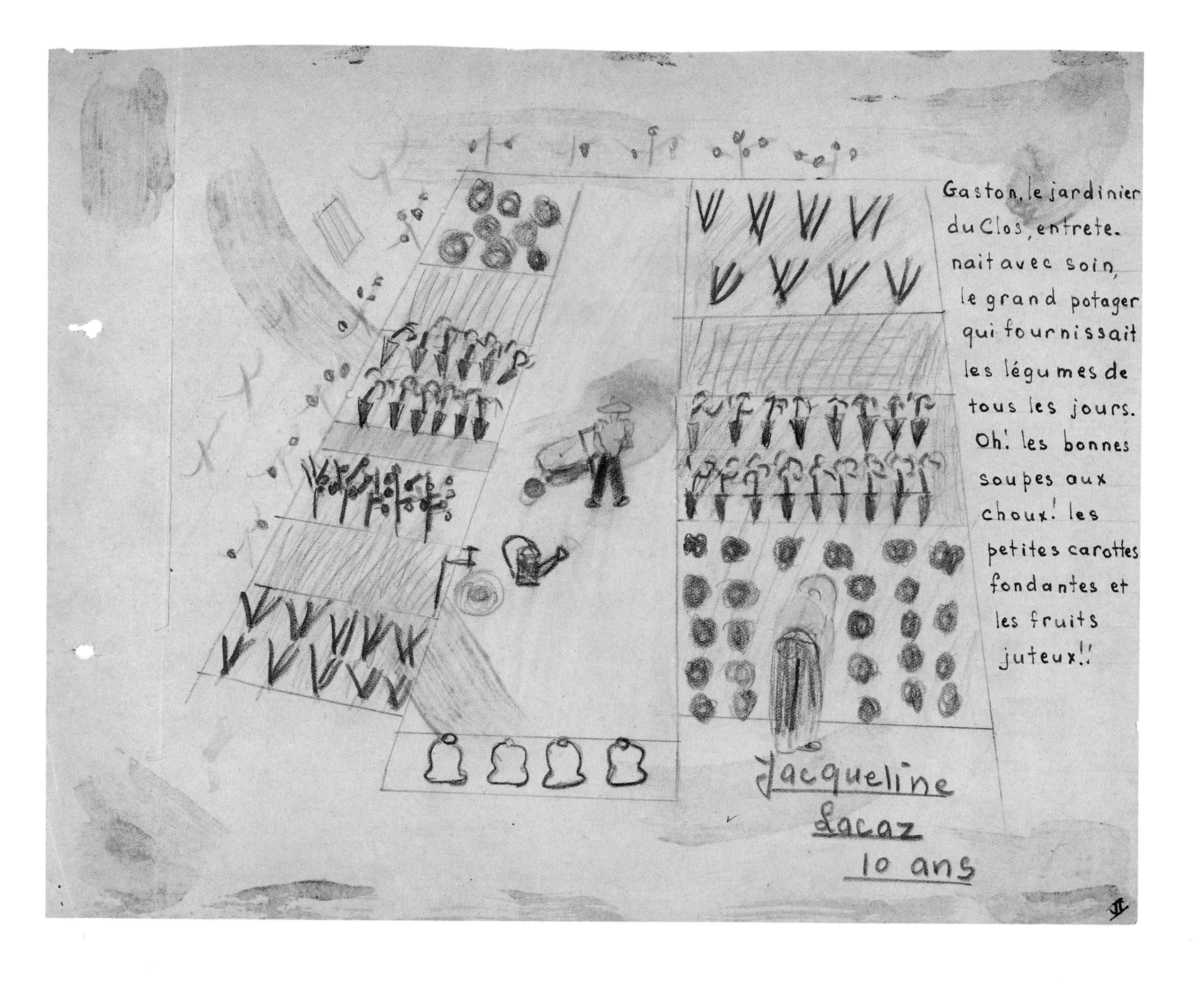
Gaston, le jardinier
du Clos, entrete-
nait avec soin,
le grand potager
qui fournissait
les légumes de
tous les jours.
Oh! les bonnes
soupes aux
choux! les
petites carottes
fondantes et
les fruits
juteux!!
Jacqueline
Lacaz
10 ans
VI

"In an enclosure near the chicken house we had many types of fowl and a house for all our rabbits."

– Denise Fernande, 12

Dans l'enclos près du poulailler, s'ébattait une nombreuse volaille, à laquelle se mêlaient tous les lapins de notre clapier.

"Under the apple trees our beautiful cows grazed.
They gave us abundant, delicious milk."

— Emma Ronquad, 12

Dans l'herbe grasse de la prairie, sous
les pommiers, paissaient nos belles va.
ches, qui nous donnaient un lait abon.
dant et dèlicieux!

cows to give them milk

"The night of June 5 and 6, 1944, at the Clos, began well. Everybody went quietly to sleep as usual, but soon we were startled awake by unusual noises. The good sleepers remained, noses in pillows, but the others dashed to the windows. They listened . . . and with a sigh of relief, they shouted, 'It's the invasion!'"

– Rose Marie Vail, 12

La nuit du 5 au 6 juin 1944, au
clos, commence bien: chacune
s'endort tranquillement comme
à l'ordinaire. Mais bientôt on
se sent tiré du sommeil malgré
soi par des bruits insolites!
Les bonnes dormeuses
demeurent le nez plongé dans
leur oreiller, mais les autres se
précipitent aux fenêtres. Elles
regardent le ciel... elles écoutent..
et avec un soupir de bonheur
s'écrient: "C'est le...
débarquement!!!
Rose Marie Vail
12 ans

"A half-mile from the entrance of the mine was a large space where the girls made their home. In spite of being underground there was enough air to breathe, and a little brook gave a certain amount of coolness. But it was black as night, and the ground was muddy. Using firewood and straw we made our beds, and here and there we hung acetylene lanterns, which were very precious in the darkness. A big wooden bench served as a table for our bread. . . . The Germans often came to search. . . . But in spite of all of the inconveniences, the little girls of the Clos felt safe in the mine where they were sheltered from the bombing."

– Monique Suret, 12

Sous la mine – A 700 mètres de l'entrée de la mine, il y a un grand espace, où
toutes les petites filles s'installent. C'est tout de même assez haut pour qu'on puisse y
respirer, et un petit ruisseau y entretient une certaine fraîcheur. Mais il y fait nuit et le sol
est boueux! A l'aide de fagots de bois et de bottes de paille, on confectionne les lits, et de
place en place on suspend une lampe à carbure, si précieuse dans notre obscurité. Un grand banc servira
de table pour poser le pain.. Ici, il faut tenir le moins de place possible, et demeurer assis plutôt que
debout. Très souvent on attendra longtemps le ravitaillement qui ne pourra arriver à cause
des obus pleuvant au dehors. Les Allemands viendront faire des fouilles. Mais malgré toutes ces
incommodités, les petites filles
du Clos sont rassu-
rées d'être sous
la mine, où
elles sont
à l'abri
des
bombarde-
ments.
Monique Suret
12 ans
XIII

"Back in the Clos, which was all but abandoned, the Germans stole and ate our poor little rabbits."

— Mauricette Bourdin, 10

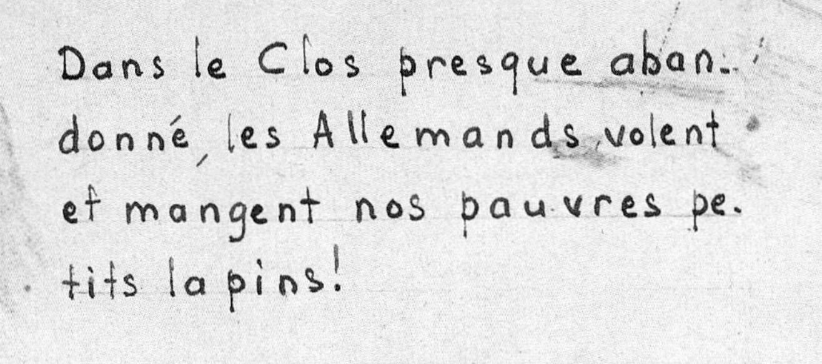
Dans le Clos presque aban-
donné, les Allemands volent
et mangent nos pauvres pe-
tits lapins!

Mauricette Bourdin
10 ans

"In the beginning of July a plane dove and bombed German trucks hidden near the Clos. Some Germans were killed; others wounded . . . the truck burned . . . and our poor mill also. . . . The Clos's two automobiles parked nearby burned too."

– Jeannine Ollichon, 12

Au début de Juillet un avion pique et bombarde la roulante allemande réfugiée près du Clos. Des Allemands sont tués, d'autres blessés.. la roulante flambe .. et notre pauvre moulin aussi! Il n'y a donc plus d'ateliers au Clos! Les deux autos du Clos garées près de là ont brûlé aussi!

"July 14. The Germans made the little girls of the Clos evacuate the mine. With no destination they took to the road . . . beneath the planes . . . under the shells. . . . Cadichon, our donkey, hauled the littlest ones who were too small to walk long distances."

– Nicole Folliot, 13

Cadichon emmène les petites qui sont trop jeunes pour marcher longtemps à pied.
Le 14 juillet les Allemands exigent que les petites filles du clos évacuent la mine. Sans destination elles prennent la route.. sous les avions.. sous les obus!..
Nicole Folliet
13 ans
XVII

"Crossing the Cinglais forest, the girls passed German tanks in flames and dead Germans. The brave little girls of the Clos followed other evacuees. All the while waving their white flags at the approaching planes."

— Odette Daigromont, 13

Cadichon emmène les petites qui sont trop jeunes pour
marcher longtemps à pied.
Le 14 juillet les Allemands
exigent que les petites filles du clos
évacuent la mine. Sans destination
elles prennent la route.. sous les avions..
sous les obus!..
Nicole Folliet
13 ans
XVII

"Crossing the Cinglais forest, the girls passed German tanks in flames and dead Germans. The brave little girls of the Clos followed other evacuees. All the while waving their white flags at the approaching planes."

— Odette Daigromont, 13

Tombes de SS
Traversée de la forêt de Cinglais, où l'on croise
des chars allemands en flammes, des Allemands
morts. Bravement les petites filles du Clos, suivent
les autres évacués. Elles ont des drapeaux blancs qu'elles
agitent à l'approche des avions.
Odette Daigremont
13 ans
XVIII

"July 15. We stopped at Acqueville in order to rest and regain our strength. As we ate lunch under the apple trees two American planes dove low and then, seeing us, climbed quickly and machine-gunned the road a little farther on. We finished our lunch with hearty appetites under the terrified eyes of the Germans."

— Yvonne Rognant, 11

15 Juillet : stationnement à Acqueville afin de reprendre des forces. Mais le déjeuner sous les pommiers est troublé par deux avions qui piquent bas. et qui, nous voyant sans doute remontent vite, et vont mitrailler la route un peu plus loin. On termine le repas de bon appétit sous l'oeil apeuré des Allemands.

"July 19. We went through Falaise silent but filled with emotion. We had to go Indian file through the streets. The girls of the Clos were astounded to see such ruins. The Germans had been driven out."

— Marcelle Blavier, 14

19 juillet. Traversée de
Falaise, émouvante et
silencieuse. Il faut faire
la file indienne pour
parcourir les rues : les petites
filles du Clos sont sidérées
de voir tant de ruines!.. Il
fallait bien dénicher
les Allemands!..
Marcelle Blavier
14 ans

"July 23. On the way to Argentan, whose spires we saw in the distance. More planes were on the prowl. . . . A convoy of British prisoners passed, and the little girls made signs to show they were friends. The planes dove but climbed again very quickly, realizing we were a friendly group of little girls in pink dresses waving our flags, but with a little shiver of fear up and down our spines."

– Jeannette Renoud, 13

23 Juillet. En route vers Argentan dont on distingue au loin les clochers! Les avions rôdent.. les voilà qui arrivent vers nous. En même temps passe sur la route un convoi de prisonniers anglais auxquels les petites filles font quelques signes d'amitié – Les avions piquent, mais remontent bien vite, se rendant compte qu'ils ont à faire à des compatriotes et à un groupe de petites filles en rose agitant bien leurs drapeaux ... avec tout de même un petit frisson de peur dans le dos.

"July 29. Now traveling in farmers' carts, the little girls of the Clos make a short stop at St. Suzanne, a picturesque little village where they are received kindly by everybody. The littlest ones joyfully drink the sweet milk served them on orders of the mayor."

– Jeannette Renaud, 13

29 Juillet. Amenées en charrettes, les petites filles du Clos, font une courte halte à Ste Suzanne, petite ville pittoresque où elles sont reçues gentiment par tout le monde. Les plus petites boivent avec joie le bon lait que le maire fait servir.

"Sometimes the little girls of the Clos slept in the welcome shelter of haylofts and haystacks, thanks to the farmers. We were glad to stretch out and sleep in the cool hay."

— Denise Fernande, 12

Au hasard des étapes, les greniers des
fermes accueillantes, abritent le sommeil
des petites filles du Clos.. qui s'étendaient
avec plaisir dans la paille fraîche.
XXIV
11ans
B. DeniseFernan

"All the way to end of their exodus, the little girls of the Clos waved their flags. They arrived at Beaufort, the end of their long trip, all safe and sound."

— Jacqueline Lacaze, 10

Jusqu'à la fin de leur exode les petites filles du
Clos agiteront leurs drapeaux. Elles arrivent, à
Beaufort, terme de leur long voyage, toutes saines et sauves!
Jacqueline
Lacoze
10 ans
XXVIII

"August 11. A few days after their arrival at Beaufort, the little girls of the Clos were happy to see American tanks. That consoled them for all that they had lost."

— Artist unknown

11 Août. Quelques jours après leur arrivée à
Beaufort, les petites filles du Clos, ont le bonheur
de voir arriver les tanks américains! Cela les console de tout
ce qu'elles ont perdu!
USA
USA

Afterword

Over a gentle hill, down a tree-lined country road, and through the open gates of a long stone wall La Maison de Clos still stands just outside of the village of St. Andre-sur-Orne. At the end of a short drive, you will see a large yellow stone house, which sits on the banks of the Orne River. Today the apple trees are overgrown and the water mill is a single ivy covered wall. Someone still cares for the garden. Le Clos is no longer a home for girls.

Moving from one place to another became a way of life for the orphans from St. Andre-sur-Orne. By 1946 they found a permanent home at Le Clos de Vaureal, a fifteenth-century chateau on the Oise River, north of Paris. The buildings and grounds were perfect for a new orphanage. But how could they pay for it? The girls were without shoes. They wore bedroom slippers because they were easy to find. They did not have beds to sleep on, so they slept on pallets stuffed with dry grass and without sheets or woolen blankets.

In 1946 Agnes Amis, a French teacher in America, received a package from her friend, Yvonne Lescure, the directress of a school in Caen, France. In the package Miss Amis found photographs of children; a small child's dress; and an illustrated journal with drawings of a large house, a garden, and a donkey. Miss Amis quickly responded to the letter from Mme. Lescure and care packages from America began to arrive at the new orphanage. Years later I sat on a small bed next to my great-aunt Aggie. She read from a journal about a war, a journey, and little girls from Normandy, while I carefully turned each page.

Yvonne Lescure and Agnes Amis in 1962

The site of the orphanage today as seen in this photo taken in 2000

A drawing of the orphanage by Nicole Folliot, 13

The orphans in Vaureal, France

Group photo of the orphans taken in Vaureal, France